MW00763902

Table of Contents

Chapter 1.. 3
Chapter 2.. 17
Chapter 3.. 27
Chapter 4.. 42
Chapter 5.. 50
Chapter 6.. 62
Chapter 7.. 73
Chapter 8.. 88
Chapter 9.. 96
Chapter 10.. 107
Chapter 11.. 119
Chapter 12.. 133
Chapter 13.. 141
Chapter 14.. 155
Chapter 15.. 165
Chapter 16.. 175
Chapter 17.. 188
Chapter 18.. 200
Chapter 19.. 209
Chapter 20.. 222

Chapter 1

"Have a beautiful day," Catherine said and handed the customer the brown paper bag. The Cat's Cookies logo peered up at her from the front – a winking cat – and she grinned.

Another perfect day in her favorite place in the world. Her very own Cookie Store.

"These Cheeky Choc Chips are selling like crazy," Lacy said and waved her hands above her head. "They can't get enough. Look at the line."

Her assistant pawed at her apron, straightened it, then cleared her throat. Lacy had a bit of an anxious streak, add the sugar habit and the recipe for disaster presented itself. This much stress couldn't be easy for her.

Cat reached over and clipped her best friend on the shoulder. "Relax. We've got plenty more where this came from. Besides, we'll just bake more tomorrow morning. Maybe a couple more of the Brittle Caramel Swirls, and we'll be good. Don't stress out about it, okay?"

Lacy pushed out her lips and wiggled them – her signature, 'not buying that' expression.

"Heya, Cat." Jeffrey stepped up to the front of the glass counter, embellished with silver, metal swirls at either end and tapped on the glass. "I'll take two of your Choc Chips to go."

"No coffee today?" Catherine asked, and peered past Jeff at the center table in the storefront. Beth hadn't come in this morning. Or maybe she had. Cat had hardly any time to chat, regardless, even if it was with the woman who'd gifted her the store.

Nerves tickled at Cat's navel – Beth hadn't missed a morning chat in the two years since she'd handed over the keys.

"Nope. I've got a big business meeting today." Jeffrey flashed a grin, then ruffled his bright, orange hair. "A contractor pulled out of the deal to build a new hotel on the waterfront. That means I'm in with a chance."

Catherine accepted his money, rang up the order, then handed him his paper baggie. "Good luck!"

"Thanks. I'll let you know how it goes."

The noise reverberated through the small space. Light filtered through the windows, from the busy street outside. Iconic buildings reared opposite Cat's Cookies, wearing their signature Capitol Street colors: beige and white. Trees poked out of holes in the brick-lined sidewalk, the wrought iron street lamps competing for space alongside them.

Charleston. Her home away from home. The only place Catherine had ever felt accepted and loved and –

"Hey, you wanna help me over here?" Lacy called, and panic seeped into her tone.

Cat spun on the spot and rushed to the faulty coffee machine in one corner. A customer stood beside Lacy and tapped her heeled boot. She checked her watch.

"This is taking forever. I'm just going to go to the Starbucks. Forget about it," the woman said, then tossed her flaxen hair back.

"Wait, please," Cat said, and closed one eye. "We've had some trouble with our coffee machine lately, but I can add a free Choc Chip cookie to your order."

"Ah, it's working!" Lacy said, and flourished her hands. She pressed a button, and the machine's milk steamer gushed hot air. "Whoops! Wrong button."

"I don't want a cookie," the woman said, and twiddled her fingers at Catherine. "I'm on a diet. Hello."

Oh, shoot. Cat couldn't relate. The minute she'd hit forty years old, she'd sworn off diets for good. What was the point – she'd rather enjoy her cookies than eat carrot sticks.

"Then you're in luck," Cat replied, and beckoned for the woman to follow her back to winding line at the front counter. "I've got just the cookie for you. A low fat, gluten-free Mojito Mint Cookie with your name written on it."

The woman eyed the counter, then glanced back at Lacy. Cat's assistant had embroiled herself in a downright war with the coffee machine. She turned, gave Cat a thumbs up, then returned to the battle.

"Here you go," Cat said and picked up a pair of antique tongs from the ledge below the counter. She slid the glass open, reached in and retrieved the Mojito Mint, then bagged it. "Enjoy." She handed the bag over.

The woman accepted it between two fingers and lifted her nose. "Thank you," she said, stiffly.

"And here's your coffee," Lacy yelled. She sprinted across the room – only twenty-year old's could sprint like that – and skidded to a halt in front of Miss Rude-pants.

The woman took that too, then fished a few dollars out of her purse and paid. She marched out of the store without another word.

"Sheesh," Lacy said, and grabbed a serviette from the pile next to the register. She dabbed at her forehead. "I hate to say it, but you're going to need to get another assistant. This place is out of control."

"Don't be dramatic," Cat said and winked at her. "We're doing just fine."

The front door opened, and customers streamed inside, yammering, clamoring, the works.

"All right," Cat said. "You might have a point."

Lacy hurried to the coffee machine and banged on it with her fist. "Don't give up on my yet," she said.

A few of the customers at the front of the line stared at her.

"May I help you?" Cat asked.

"Three Cheeky Choc Chips," the old woman replied.

"Coming right up!" Cat cared about three things: cookies, Oreo her mischievous pet kitty, and her friends.

Lacy and Beth were family to her. The only family she'd ever had.

"Would you like a coffee with that?" Cat asked.

Lacy banged on the coffee machine again, then pressed a button. Hot water dribbled from the nozzle and onto the grate next to the Styrofoam cup.

The woman paid and accepted the bag. She eyed the ongoing war at the coffee station. "No, thank you."

A police officer stepped up to the counter next, decked out in his lawman blues. His bright green gaze landed on the counter, then flicked to her face. "Mrs. Kelley?"

"That's Miss, and what can I get you, officer?" Cat asked.

He ruffled his dirty blonde hair at the back of his head. "I need to ask you a couple of questions," he replied. He sure had that handsome detective thing going on.

"Questions? Uh, I'm a little busy right now, officer. We're in the middle of the brunch rush."

"Why won't you work?" Lacy growled and pressed more buttons on the coffee machine.

"I'm afraid this can't wait, Miss Kelley. We need to talk. In private."

Cat stepped back from the counter and brushed off her palms on her apron. "I hope it's nothing serious."

The officer's expression didn't alter a whit. Gray flecked the blond hairs at his temples. A frown wrinkled his tan brow.

"Lacy. Forget the coffee for a second. Put up an out of order sign on the machine and man the counter. I'll be back in five," Cat said.

Her assistant hurried to the counter.

The officer nodded once and walked to the side of the room, to the spot beside the stairs which led up to Cat's home above the store. He didn't look happy.

"Make that ten minutes," she whispered, and a deep sense of

foreboding settled on her shoulders.

Chapter 2

Catherine sat down on her checked sofa and gestured for the officer to take a seat on the armchair beside her old TV set. He didn't sit down, but he flashed a small, tight smile.

It slipped off his face like cookie crumbs off a toddler's fingers.

"Should I be worried, officer, uh. I'm sorry, I didn't catch your name?"

"Detective Jack Bradshaw," he said, and folded his arms. He stared her down.

"Well, I would introduce myself, but you already know my name, where I work and where I live," Cat said and chuckled. A nervous, squeak of a laugh.

She'd never spoken to an officer; other than the time she'd gotten a speeding ticket. Innocent mistake, she'd missed a turn-off and continued at the same speed but –

"I'm afraid I have some bad news," the Detective said.

Cat interlaced her fingers and placed her hands on her knees. Oreo wandered through the door which led into the kitchen, and meowed once. He turned yellow eyes on the newcomer, then padded to the sofa.

He hopped up, then crawled into Cat's lap and proceeded to needle massage her lap. Needle massage – her nickname for the clawing he did each time he fell asleep.

"Cut it out, Oreo," she whispered, and nudged him back.

"Miss Kelley," Detective Bradshaw said. "I regret to inform you that Beth Walters is dead."

The sofa crashed into her back. No, she'd collapsed against it. She sucked in great, big gasps. Shock trembled through her legs. "No," she said. Oreo's weight pinned her to the sofa.

Bradshaw's tough expression wavered, but he slammed regained his composure. "Miss Walters fell off the pier in the early hours of this morning at the Waterfront Park. She was found —"

"Impossible," Cat said.

"Pardon me?"

"That's impossible. Beth was obsessed with fishing. She's spent more time fishing off that pier than she has eating cookies in my store. She was an experienced swimmer too." Sure, Cat's benefactor had been nearly seventy, but she'd had the constitution of a thirty-year-old.

Detective Bradshaw unfolded his arms. He stared at her, weighing her like flour on the scale. "Mrs. Walters appears to have been knocked on the back of the head, prior to falling into the water. Blunt force trauma is the official term."

Cat pressed her palms to her eyes to block it out. Beth. Her Beth. The woman who'd helped her set herself up after she'd arrived in Charleston fresh out of a corporate position she'd despised. And she was gone?

"I don't want to believe this. No one I knew would want to hurt Beth. She was an amazing person," Cat said, and finally dropped her hands.

Jack Bradshaw brought his notepad and pen out of his pocket. "Beth's family, a Mr. Joseph Walters and Mrs. Tara Walters, has informed us that her will had been changed at the last moment," he said.

"Where are you going with this?" Catherine asked, and narrowed her eyes.

"They've informed us that you are the sole benefactor of Mrs. Walter's inheritance."

"What? That's – wait, you don't think I had something to do with this?" Cat asked, then stood up straight as an arrow.

Oreo hissed and landed on the floorboards, then padded off. He flicked his tail at her.

"Because that's plain ridiculous. I had no interest in Beth's money. She was my friend. No, she was family," Catherine said.

"Is it true that she gave you this building?"

"Yeah, but what's that –?"

"How did you persuade Mrs. Walters to give it to you?" Bradshaw asked and clicked his ballpoint pen.

Cat's jaw dropped. She snapped it closed, then squared her shoulders. "I don't appreciate this line of questioning, Detective."

"Answer the question."

"She was an old friend of my mother's. I met up with her after my parent's passed. She knew I had a passion for baking and wanted to help me set myself up —"

"So, she just gave it to you?" Bradshaw asked.

"Yes! She was a giving human being." Which was more than she could've said for this guy. "I'll tell you something else. Beth hardly ever saw her relatives."

"Why not?" The Detective asked.

Cat's irritation had peaked. "Because they tried to siphon money out of her. They didn't care about who she was. They just saw her as the wealthy grandmother. A walking payday." The gall of those people, accusing her.

"I see," Detective Bradshaw said. Though, it didn't seem like it. "I think that's all I need, for now, Miss Kelley. I'll be in touch." He turned and walked to the door, his shoes clicking on the wood.

Catherine ground her teeth and glared at his back. "Aren't you going to tell me not to leave town?"

He paused a foot from the exit and looked back over his shoulder. "Don't worry, Miss

Kelley. I'm good at what I do. If you left, I'd find you."

And then he strode from the room and out of her apartment. The front door slammed shut behind him.

Chapter 3

Cat stood outside the Walters residence, grasping a folded cardboard box of Cheek Choc Chip cookies. The two-story house glared down at her. The veiled windows disapproved of her presence, and Catherine squared her shoulders

"This place is fancy," Lacy said and readjusted her black skirt and pillbox hat. "It's like a mansion, not a house."

An outside door opened on the upstairs patio and a blonde woman, draped in pearls, stepped up to the railing. She matched the house's empty stare and sneered at them.

"Cat? Maybe we shouldn't have come. Given what they said about you, this isn't exactly going to be a pleasant –"

"Beth was more our family than she was theirs, Lace. We're doing this. I wouldn't miss her memorial service for the world." And if she discovered why the Walters family had accused her of murder at the same time, all the better.

"Okay, I just know you're angry, and when you get mad, you can get a little boisterous."

Catherine cleared her throat and stepped onto the stone paved path which led to the sweeping front porch. "I'm not angry. I'm enraged. There's a minuscule difference."

Lacy puffed her cheeks out.

"Relax, I promise I won't do anything. I outgrew temper tantrums at three," she said and popped up a smile for her young friend's benefit. The first smile since she'd discovered Beth had passed.

No, she'd been murdered and whoever had done it wanted it to seem like she was the culprit.

Catherine stepped onto the bottom stair. Lacy joined her. They nodded to each other, then traversed the staircase and halted in front of the door. It stood ajar, and a cool breeze wafted past them.

"Candles," Lacy said, and wriggled her nose.

"Excuse me?"

"I smell candles," Lace replied. She had the nose of a blood hound.

Catherine moved across the threshold and followed the sound of chatter, down a long wooden hall. Family portraits lined the walls – images of four people: a surly day, that same pearl-bedecked woman, a young boy and a girl who'd shifted away from the other three slightly. Not exactly the image of a happy family.

"Here we go," Cat said and turned into the living room.

People milled around the space, eating savory snacks and drinking cool sodas and pink lemonade. An image of Beth sat on top of a Grand Piano in the corner – the photo had probably been taken years ago, but Cat couldn't reconcile the woman in the picture with the one she'd come to love as a second mother.

The Walters had chosen a straight-laced photograph. Beth had been anything but straight-laced. She'd dyed her hair purple for heaven's sake.

A few of the guests glanced up and spotted her. They fell silent. That quiet spread across the room. People turned and stared, narrowed their eyes, shook their heads.

"Told you," Lacy whispered. "What did I tell you?"

"Practice your breathing, Lace."

Lacy sucked in air through her nose and breathed gently out her mouth. She snorted a couple of times in between. A few of the guests shifted their gazes to her, instead. That didn't help Lacy's panic. Her breathing exercises turned into a mini-hyperventilation attack.

"What are those?" A woman asked, behind them.

They turned on the spot – Lace complexion colored a lovely shade of mauve – and blinked at the young, uh, lady.

"They're Choc Chip cookies from my bakery," Cat said. She didn't want to be rude, but this girl's hair and makeup reminded her of something out of the Rocky Horror Picture Show.

The college student swept bright, pink locks back from her forehead, and slouched against the wall beside the door.

Eyeshadow blackened her lids, and she'd smeared on dark lipstick to match it.

Lacy's mauve color paled to a rosy pink.

The chatter behind them swelled again – no doubt she'd triggered a festival of gossip on arrival.

Cat stepped up to the girl, wearing a tight grin. "I'm Catherine Kelley, but you can call me Cat. What's your name?"

The woman didn't extend a hand. "I'm Rachel Walters." She folded her arms and eyed the box of cookies in Cat's hands.

"You want one?" She asked, and popped the lid, then held them out to the skinny, young lady bedecked in black velvets. So, this was a member of the famed Walter's family. She didn't seem that bad.

She probably hadn't started that rumor about Cat being the killer, though. Or had she?

Catherine jiggled the cookie box at the girl.

"Thanks," Rachel said and grinned. She leaned in and snatched up a treat, then crunched it between her lips. "Mom's got me on this crazy diet ever since I got back from college."

"Oh yeah?"

"Yeah. She wants me to be little miss perfect you know? I am so not that kind of girl."

Lacy took a cookie and inhaled it for the sugar rush. She licked the crumbs off her fingers. "What are you studying?" She asked.

"I'm, ugh, hate it. Pre-law." Rachel snorted and twirled a finger at her head. "Can you picture me as a lawyer? I don't think so."

Catherine didn't help herself to a cookie. "So, you didn't get on with your parents?"

"Nope. They're all high society. Lame. I swear, the only person who understood me in this entire family was Gramma Beth," Rachel said, then reached for another choc chip. "I can't believe she's gone now."

"You were close to her?" Catherine asked. This was useful information. Maybe she could call that handsome and slightly rude detective and give him a few leads for his case.

She couldn't have the whole of Charleston under the impression that she'd murdered the darling of the town.

"We were close since I got back from college. She took me fishing a few times. It was weird. I've never been fishing before," Rachel said, between bites of cookie. "These are so good, by the way –"

"Rachel," a man snapped. He stepped through the open arch which led into the living room, then smoothed his crisp, black suit. "What are you doing?"

"Just what you told me, dad. Chilling. Acting normal. That's what you said, isn't it?" Rachel narrowed her eyes at him and pouted.

"Go to the bathroom and take off that ridiculous makeup," Mr. Walters said, then grabbed the half-eaten cookie from her. He threw it back into the Cat's Cookies box.

"Hey," Cat said. "There's no need to be rude. She was just –"

"Now," Walters said and pointed out of the doorway.

Rachel shrugged and pressed her lips into a thin, black line. "I'll see ya around," she whispered, then hurried from the room.

"That was uncalled for," Cat said.

"Your presence is uncalled for," Mr. Walters replied, and folded his arms. He stared down his nose at her. "You will leave now."

"Excuse me?"

"You will leave my premises now. You're not welcome here," Walters growled.

"I —"

"If you don't leave in the next five seconds, I'm going to call the police."

Cat stared at Mr. Walters, anger burning through her mind. How dare he treat her like this? She'd come to pay her respects to Beth. She'd —

"Five," he said, and shifted on the spot, distributing his weight, evenly. "Four."

"All right, all right. Keep your toupee on," Cat replied. "Come on, Lace. Let's get out of this coffin and into the sun."

"Coffin!" Mr. Walters gasped and pressed his palm to his chest.

Cat didn't give him a chance to strike up another bout of reprimands. She tucked her arm through Lacy's and led her assistant down the hall and onto the front porch.

Chapter 4

"What a horrible dude. And I think you're right about the hair piece. Nobody has hair that glossy," Lacy said, and turned her face to the sun. They stood on the sidewalk, in front of the white Walter's mansion.

Cat burned for answers. Shoot, she pined for them. Walters was either convinced she'd hurt Beth, or didn't want her around for another reason. Keeping up appearances? Hiding something?

She had to know.

"No," Lacy said, in a long drawn out groan.

"What?"

She peered into Cat's face. "You've got that look again. You've got that look you get before you do something crazy."

"Not crazy. I'm just going to go back in there and take a look around."

Lacy buried her face in her palm. "That's the definition of crazy, I swear. He'll catch you and then the cops will come and then you'll end up in jail. And I don't have money for bail, Cat. I have student loans to pay off. You can't. Please, I –"

"Lacy, breathe. Just breathe." Cat grasped her forearm, unable to tear her gaze from the open front door. "Have I ever let you down before?"

"No, but –"

"Have I ever gotten you into a sticky situation that you couldn't get out of?"

"There was the one time, with the cookie dough and that group of kids at the charity event," Lacy said.

Cat rolled her eyes. "You'll never let me forget that."

"Oreo won't either," Lacy replied, and started her hyperventilating again.

Cat released her friend's arm, then brushed off the modest black silk blouse and tailored pants she'd chosen for the service. Music started up inside. A tune played on the piano.

"Is that... Hallelujah?" Lacy asked, between breaths.

"Here," Cat said, and shoved the box of cookies into her hands. "I'll be right back."

"But —"

"Wait in the car and keep a low profile." Cat darted up the front path and onto the porch, then stepped into the cool interior for the second time in the span of ten minutes.

Voices rose in a chorus in the living room. Everyone was distracted.

Beth's true murderer could be in that room at this very moment, pretending to care about a woman who'd cared about everyone and everything.

Cat balled her hands into fists, then took off up the main flight of stairs. She hit the second floor landing and glanced left and right. Her heart pounded against the inside of her ribcage and she held her breath.

Footsteps stomped down the hall, around the corner.

"Shoot," Cat whispered, then rushed into the room directly opposite the stairs. She squeaked the door shut behind her, and pressed her ear to it. Silence. Apart from the rush of blood in her head, of course.

Catherine forced out a sigh of relief, then turned and pressed her back against the pale wood. Her eyes widened. Her rush to find information of use had led her directly into…

"The study?"

Bookshelves lined the far wall, stacked with dusty books, their spines faded by the sunlight which streamed through an open window. Cars rushed by outside.

Cat walked to the shelves and narrowed her eyes at the titles and author names. Shakespeare, Tolkien, Jordan, Hemingway, Hiaasen. An eclectic mix of authors and books, but none of them had been touched in ages.

Apparently, the Walters weren't readers.

"Wait, what's that?" Cat muttered.

One of the books had a dust-free spine. She slipped it out from the end of the row, then frowned at the plain, leather cover. No title.

"Intriguing." She flipped back the cover, then slipped her fingers between the vellum pages. She opened the book on the first page, then gasped.

Death. Death. Death. Death. Death.

The word scrawled across the pages in black ink. Cat paged through it, and her stomach turned. Every single page carried the words. Over and over again. Handwritten, scraped into the page at some parts.

Cat closed it and gripped the journal between her fingertips. They turned white from the pressure.

Whoever had written it, clearly had an obsession. This was her first piece of solid evidence.

Chapter 5

Music blared through the old TV set, a tune to match the Venetian waltz.

Cat shook out her arms, then held them in a stiff frame. She raised her head, lowered her shoulders, and stared at the thick, fabric of her curtains.

"And, on the count of three, we'll begin," the woman on the screen said.

Butterflies fluttered in Cat's belly. She'd bought the dance DVD ages ago, but she hadn't mastered the Venetian waltz. She hadn't come close.

"One," the woman said.

Oreo meandered through the living room door and froze, mid-step. He flicked his tail once.

He hated it when she did dance practice without him. Or maybe he hated it that she'd moved his favorite armchair out of the way to provide more floor space.

"Two."

Oreo meowed at her, then sat down and gave her two flicks of the tail.

"Not now, Oreo, I'm trying to figure this out." The two things that calmed her after a stressful day were dance and baking cookies. She'd already baked a ton of cookies to get rid of the memory of reading that death book and speaking to Mr. Walters.

"Three."

The music started fresh, and Cat launched into the slow, sweeping steps of the waltz. She traveled and turned, grinning at the invisible audience.

If someone glanced through her window, now, they'd think she was a loon.

Oreo blinked up at her, then meowed again.

"Give me a break, Oreo. You just had your milk." Cat changed direction and swept toward the TV, instead.

Another meow, louder this time.

Catherine stumbled and flung her arms out. She caught the edge of the tiny bookshelf, and it wobbled. The leather-bound journal dropped out and landed face down on the floorboards.

"Great," Cat said. "Just what I wanted to see, right now."

Oreo meowed for the millionth time.

"Fine, fine, fine. What do you want, kitty?" Catherine asked.

Oreo stopped wagging his tail, immediately. He rose onto all fours then padded down the hall.

"Oreo?" Cat grabbed the remote and paused her DVD. "Hey, what are you up to?"

He meowed back at her.

Catherine strode across the room, then stopped beneath the lintel. "What's gotten into you?"

Oreo stood at the gate which separated her apartment from the top of the stairs which led right down into the bakery. He paced across the entrance, then turned a circle on top of a slip of paper on the polished wooden boards.

"What?" Catherine frowned, then hurried to Oreo's side. She bent and stroked his fur, smoothing the black fluff back. She twirled his tail between her fingertips, and he purred and rubbed against her shins.

She lifted the square of paper, then opened it on its center fold.

You will pay, or you will die.

Cat gasped, and it shuddered through her chest and down her arms. Her fingers trembled. She ran them across the neatly inked words and read the text again. "Pay?" She asked. She had nothing to pay off.

No debts or unpaid loads. Unless she had to pay in another way. But for what?

Catherine rose, slowly, gaze glued to the page. Oreo twirled between her legs, purring and meowing.

"I'm okay, Oreo. Thanks," she said, absently. She glanced down at the bottom of the stairs, but the bakery was quiet.

She'd locked up the front and back ages ago. Shoot, it was already past 9 PM.

Cold shivers ran up and down her spine. Someone had been in her bakery because the note certainly hadn't been on the landing when she'd come up earlier.

"A break-in?" Catherine bit her bottom lip, then grabbed the door handle and slammed her front door closed. She turned the key in the lock, then slammed the bolt into place for good measure.

The clack of metal on metal didn't give her much comfort.

The person who'd left the message could still be downstairs. "It's a lure," Cat said. "They want me to go downstairs and check it out. They'll probably try to overwhelm me if I do."

Oreo meowed and sat down beside her foot.

"Don't worry, Oreo, I'm not going down there. I'm impulsive, but even I have my limits." Cat lifted the note and examined the text again. That was it! The text.

She darted back down the hall and into the living room. She ignored the dance instructor, frozen on the TV screen, and snatched the creepy, fallen death journal from the floor.

She flipped it open, then placed the letter on one of the pages and spread it open.

Catherine squinted and compared the text. "Nope," she whispered. "Not the same handwriting." That didn't tell her much.

Catherine placed the book and the note on top of her shelves, then paced back to the sofa. She sat down and folded her hands in her lap. Oreo galloped through from the hall and leaped onto the sofa cushions.

"No needle massages today, kitty," Catherine said. "I need to think."

Beth was gone. A murderer was on the loose, and the cops thought she'd committed the crime.

"That's it," she whispered. She grabbed her cellphone off the sofa, then dialed a number she'd saved under emergency contacts, two years ago.

"Charleston Police Department," a man said, on the other end of the line. His gruff voice didn't instill much hope.

"Hi there, I need to speak with Detective Jack Bradshaw. It's in connection with the murder of Beth Walters."

"Uh, just one moment please," the officer replied.

A shrill tune squeaked across the line. Catherine held the phone away from her ear and stared at the journal on top of the bookshelf.

"Hello?"

Cat placed the phone against her ear again. "Detective Bradshaw?

This is Cat Kelley. Someone just broke into my house and left me a threatening message. I think it's in connection with Beth's murder."

The detective sniffed then cleared his throat. "I'm on my way."

Chapter 6

Detective Jack Bradshaw held the note at arm's length and squinted at it. He tilted his head from one side, then swapped the angle out to the other.

"Is everything okay?" Cat asked.

"Yeah, fine. I forgot my reading glasses," the Detective said and gave a sheepish grin. He zipped it off his lips a second later.

Bradshaw had arrived at the bakery in record time. Not ten minutes after she'd made the call had passed, and he'd rapped his knuckles on the front door downstairs. Only then, had she been brave enough to go down into the bakery and open up for him.

"I'm sorry, I don't have any reading glasses. Otherwise, I'd give them to you," Catherine said.

"No, no, it's fine. I'll have to take this to the station, though. It's evidence." Detective Bradshaw folded it up and placed it on top of the coffee table. He glanced at the TV and the dance instructor frozen mid-step. His eyebrows did a dance, but he didn't say a word.

"That's it?" Catherine asked. "You're just going to take the note in? What about the break-in? There could be someone in the bakery, right now."

Bradshaw pursed his lips. "Right. You stay here. I'll go check it out. Give me five minutes." He walked out of the room and down the hall before she could reply.

Catherine shook her head. Manners clearly weren't Jack Bradshaw's strong point. She rose from the sofa and crossed to the bookshelf, then lifted the 'death journal' from the top.

She turned it over in her hands and stroked the leather cover. This was her only piece of evidence now. She had to figure out who'd killed Beth, not just for herself, but for the woman who'd given her hope in her darkest moments.

Cat tucked the book against her chest. "This is personal."

Jack's footsteps clomped up the stairs. Catherine hurried back to the sofa, then shoved the journal beneath one of the cushions. She sat down on top of it and crossed her ankles.

Detective Bradshaw entered the living room and clicked off his flashlight. "No one in the bakery," he said. "But I found the back door wide open."

"That's impossible. I locked it this evening."

"Are you sure?" Detective Bradshaw asked, in a monotone.

"Because the lock wasn't broken."

"I am positive, detective." Cat glanced at the curtains which obscured the road from view. She shut her eyes for a second, then opened them and focused her gaze on Bradshaw's. "Someone's trying to pin this murder on me."

"It's too early to make those kinds of assumptions, Miss Kelley."

"Call me Cat," she said, then blinked. "And it's not too early. That note insinuates as much."

Jack touched his palm to his top pocket. "I'll have to examine it back at the station, Miss Kelley."

"Cat."

"I believe you attended Mrs. Walter's memorial service?" He asked, and tucked his arms behind his back.

Catherine kept a straight face. "Yeah, I attended, all right. And the Walters were exceptionally rude to me. Beth was my best friend. No, she was more than that. Obviously, I attended the service."

Jack Bradshaw bobbed his chin up and down, once. He opened his mouth to say something. Another question, no doubt.

"You said Beth was hit over the head and pushed off the pier?" Cat asked.

Bradshaw snapped his mouth shut. "Yes, that's correct but –"

"And you don't have the murder weapon?"

"No, not yet, but it looks like she was hit with something heavy. Perhaps, a tackle box," Jack said. His cheeks colored and he clicked his teeth together.

"A tackle box? Does that mean your main suspect is a fisherman? Or a fisherwoman?" Cat asked. She'd never questioned anyone before. It was fun. Intimidating, but fun.

"No," Jack replied.

"Then why do you suspect a tackle box to be the murder

weapon? What information led you to believe that?" Cat asked, and put up a smile – the brightest she could muster while talking about her friend's murder.

"We've had some reports of a stranger hanging around the pier," Bradshaw said. His eyes widened, and he pressed his lips together.

"A stranger?"

"That's enough," the detective said. "This is an ongoing investigation, and I'm not at liberty to share that kind of information with you. Is that understood?"

Catherin sighed. She had pushed him a little far. But that extra push had just given her a new lead. "I'm sorry, detective. I didn't mean to put you in an awkward position."

He brushed off his dark blue shirt, the corners of his lips twitching into a smile. "That's, it's, yes, it's all right."

"Thank you for coming out here," Cat said. She'd been pretty freaked at the thought of a stranger in her bakery.

"It's what I do," the detective replied. "I'll see myself out, Miss Kelley. There' no need to come downstairs."

"Thanks," Cat said and glanced at the TV.

"Yeah, I'll leave you with your dance lessons," he said, and his mouth twitched again. An almost smile.

His almost smile was cute.

Cat shook her head to get that thought out. "Good night, detective," she said.

"Miss Kelley," he grunted, then turned and marched back down the hall. The door closed a second later, then the gate after that. His footsteps echoed down the stairs and into the bakery.

Oreo hopped into her lap and settled. His purr radiated through her sweats, and she stroked his velvety ears.

"The pier," Cat whispered. "That's our next lead, Oreo. We've got to get down there and find out what happened." She practiced a few breathing exercises, then leaned her head against the sofa cushions. This was ridiculous. She couldn't let a little break-in, and a strange note set her on edge.

Tomorrow, she'd go back to the scene of the crime. What would Bradshaw think about that?

Chapter 7

Lacy and Cat stood shoulder to shoulder, staring at the slatted bench.

"This is it?" Lacy asked.

"Yeah, this was her favorite bench. She used to come here on days like this. Sunny Saturdays," Catherine replied, then sighed and ran a hand through her shoulder-length dark hair.

"I can't believe she's gone," Lacy replied.

The crash of waves against the rocks interrupted her sentence. Lacy stepped up to the bench, then turned and sat down. She looked out at the ocean, and a salty breeze tussled her short-cut red locks. She shivered, then pointed out at the pier.

Catherine followed her gaze.

Three or four men stood huddled together on the end of the stone and wood construction, their fishing poles on their shoulders.

"Is that where it happened?" Lacy asked.

"I can't be sure. But it was somewhere here. And that means the killer was here too," Cat replied. She narrowed her eyes at the huddle of fishermen, then sniffed. The strong tang of fish hit her olfactory cells full on. "Wow. Kinda fresh out here."

"Tell me about it," Lacy replied.

Catherine strolled down the wooden walkway and folded her arms against her pale yellow cardigan. The men on the pier hadn't noticed her, yet.

"Hey, wait for me," Lacy said. She rushed up beside Cat and tapped her on the arm. "You can't just leave me back there. I mean, there's a killer on the loose, right? What if he decided I was next? What if –?"

"The sky fell on your head?"

"Ha-ha, very funny," Lacy said.

"If you continue freaking out like that I'm going to start calling you Chicken Little." Catherine linked arms with her friend and led her down the dock.

Seagulls cawed overhead, scoping the area for a quick bite to eat. They swept down and landed on the end of the pier, white and black bodies far too fat for scavengers.

Beth had loved them. She'd fed them bait, and bits of fish and other gross tidbits Cat hadn't asked about. Bleh.

The women turned onto the pier, then strolled down.

Shouts reached their ears. The fishermen huddle didn't budge, but the men glared at each other across the short distance which separated them.

"I didn't touch the old lady. She was my friend too, George. You've lost your tackle if you think I have it in me to –"

"Uh huh?" The shorter guy asked, and tapped his heel on the rough boards. "Then how come you were the last one to leave the pier the other night, when she was here. Huh? Explain that. I bet you did do it. You should be ashamed of yourself. She was a saint!"

"She reminded me of my great grandma," another man said, and dabbed a crusty handkerchief beneath his lower eyelids.

"She was everyone's grandma," the short man yelled.

"Keep it down," the final fisherman said, a portly guy in a loose shirt. He pointed at Cat and Lacy. "We've got company."

The men turned to face them, and Lacy tugged on Cat's arm. But Cat didn't stop moving. She walked right up to the group and flashed them her brightest smile. "Hi," she said, "I'm Catherine Kelley."

"We know who you are," the tall man said. The guy who'd been accused of hurting Beth. "We heard that you're the one that's getting all Beth's money."

"I'm not," Cat replied. She hadn't heard anything about a will or money, apart from accusations, and she didn't care, for that matter. "I was one of Beth's closest friend's though."

"Bob," the tall man said, and extended a grimy hand.

Cat shook it. Lacy grimaced.

"George." That came from the short man. "The fat guy is Bill, and the weepy guy is Leonard."

"They're like the seven dwarves," Lacy said, "only there's four of them."

"Who are you calling a dwarf?" George replied, and drew himself up straight. He shifted the fishing pole against his shoulder.

"Oh no," Lace said, "I didn't mean it like that. I just meant –"

Cat waved a hand to draw attention from the fishermen – and to take the heat off her best friend. "I'm investigating Beth's murder."

"You're not a cop," George said and folded his stubby arms. "Show me your badge."

"You're absolutely right, George," Catherine replied. The wind whisked her hair around her face, and it whipped her across the nose. She hooked it back behind her ear. "I'm not a cop. But the cops think I did it, and I loved Beth with all my heart."

"Oh, Beth," Leonard wailed, then dabbed at his eyes again.

"So, you didn't kill her, then?" Bill asked, and adjusted the hem of his pants around his expansive girth.

"Of course, she killed her," George yelled. "She'd say anything to get out of it."

"A second ago, you said I killed her," Bob replied, and lifted a finger into the air. "Everyone shut up and listen to what this nice lady has to say."

George pouted and examined the end of his fishing pole. "Fine."

"Right," Cat said and searched her thoughts. She had to get back on track after the interruption. "Right, so as I was saying, I've taken to investigating."

"So you can pin the murder on someone else," George grumbled, and Bob slapped him on the back. He made an 'oof' noise, then shut his mouth.

"I wanted to find out if you guys had seen anything suspicious around here, in the weeks leading up to Beth's murder." A bitter taste spread on Cat's tongue. The word murder didn't fit into her vocabulary.

"I didn't see nothing," George replied.

Bill let out a massive burp and Lacy recoiled, then pressed her palm to her mouth.

"Anyone else?" What if they didn't speak to her because she didn't have a badge? That would make her little mini-investigation even more difficult.

Bob raised his arm. "I saw a stranger hanging around the day before Beth's murder. Short, bald guy."

"You sure you're not talking about this stranger?" Bill asked, and jerked his thumb toward George.

The short man growled low in his throat, then pointed to the tufts of gray hair which encircled the naked patch of skin at his crown. "Do I look bald to you?"

Bob ignored them. "I tried speaking to him. We're fishermen. We stick together around here. But this guy, sheesh, he didn't want anything to do with us. He just gave me this real creepy lookin' grin then wandered off. He spoke to Beth, though."

"He talked to Beth? Did she tell you what it was about?" Cat asked.

"Nope, but she didn't like him either. I could tell from the look on her face." Bob stood his fishing pole straight and placed the end on the wooden boards. "Didn't catch his name either, but I haven't seen him around since Beth since she —"

Leonard burst into a fresh set of sobs, again.

"Thank you, Bob, that's helpful." Cat stepped back and waved to them. "I've got to go now, but I'll let you know what else I find out. And hey, if you guys like cookies, you should stop by my store on Monday. I'll fix you up with something good."

"You got any of those ginger cookies?" Bill called after her.

"You bet," she replied, and gave him a thumbs up.

She grasped Lacy's arm, then walked back down the pier. Her hair whipped around her head, tangled by the salty breeze.

"That was… an experience," Lacy said. "I thought I'd die when he burped."

Cat rolled her eyes. "C'mon," she said. "All this investigating has given me an appetite. Let's go to the farmer's market and check out the produce."

"That's the best idea I've heard in weeks. Apart from the Choc Mudslide Cookie, of course," Lacy replied.

"Of course." But Cat couldn't get the image of the strange, short man out of her thoughts. Another lead, and another suspect. The cookie dough got stickier by the minute.

Chapter 8

Barbequed ribs sizzled on the griddle and the sweet honey scent filled the air around the stall. Cat and Lacy stood in the long line, in front of it, drooling for a taste.

"Wow," Lacy said. "I'm never skipping a farmer's market again. This place is unbelievable."

Rows of stalls lined the walkways. Families wandered between them, shopping everything from potted plants to homemade canned sauces to trout jerky. Smells and sounds filled the area.

A wash of culture and color and – oh boy, it was just Cat's favorite place to be, apart from Cat's Cookies, of course.

"We can get something to eat, then take a look around. I wonder if they have any cat toys here," Catherine said and placed her index finger under her chin. "I need to get something for Oreo."

"What about the Halloween pumpkin ball I got him last year?"

"Oh, he's already scratched through that. He loved it so much. He wouldn't let it out of his sight. The poor thing has gone from orange to yellow to beige."

"The fluffy pumpkin ball or Oreo?" Lacy asked, and arched an eyebrow.

"Oreo's still as black as ever, I assure you," Cat replied.

The line shifted forward a few steps, and they hurried to close the gap. The sooner they got their order in, the better. Cat's belly grumbled a complaint.

"Fancy meeting you here, murderer," a man said, behind her.

Lacy and Catherine froze. They stared at each other, then turned to face the man.

A young guy – with a full head of hair, shoot – stood behind them in the line, arms folded across his blue Polo shirt. "I didn't know killers enjoyed the farmer's market, like regular folk."

This kid had to be just out of high school. So much for respecting elders, right?

"Who are you?" Catherine asked. She looked up at the young man and schooled herself to calm.

"I'm Kevin Walters. You killed my grandmother," he said, loudly.

A couple of the people in line for the ribs turned and craned their necks back down the line.

Lacy tried to shrink back, but there wasn't space.

"Well, Kevin Walters, you might want to work on your manners. How old are you? Nineteen? Younger?"

"That's none of your business," he said, a snarl curled his upper lip. "I don't fraternize with murderers."

"Look, I know your parents probably raised you to believe that you're everything. You're a star, right? Take on the world and all that, but you need to learn some respect. A bad attitude will get you nowhere, fast," Catherine replied.

Lacy sucked in a couple of breaths, then squared her shoulders. "Yeah."

"What, is this your bodyguard?" The kid asked, and pointed to Lace.

"Is there a reason you approached me, child?" Catherine asked, and gave him her sweetest smile. "I was in the middle of a conversation before you interrupted."

"Man, what kind of idiot was my grandmother to leave her money to a woman like you. What are you going to do with it? Spend it on ribs and cookies and all kinds of junk," the kid replied.

That was it. If Cat hadn't been in control of her faculties, she might've shaken this kid for a comment like that. "Beth Walters was an incredible human being," Cat replied. "I wouldn't expect you to understand that. Goodbye."

She turned her back on Kevin and moved forward in the line. Only two people ahead of them, and then they'd have their ribs. She focused on that, to avoid the bubbling anger in her gut.

How dare he accuse her of murdering Beth? And worse, how dare he speak about his grandmother like that?

"He's gone," Lacy said, after a second. "And he didn't look happy about leaving. I don't think he came for the barbecued ribs, though."

"No, he came to make a point. Or to do someone else's dirty work." Cat stepped to the front table and eyed the ribs on the grill. "I'll have two of your largest portions, please."

She'd need to keep her strength up for what came next. Catherine Kelley was anything but a coward, and Kevin had invoked a deep sense of determination within her.

Chapter 9

Crickets chirped in the bushes beneath the window. Catherine crouched between the leaves and held her breath. She let it out slowly, a long, low exhale, then crept along the side of the Walters' residence.

Impulsive. That was what Lacy called her. Beth had once said her body knew what Cat wanted to do before her brain did.

"Boy, I hope I don't regret this," Cat whispered. This was the first time she'd ever crab-walked outside someone's home past eight o'clock at night.

She stopped beneath a bottom floor window – probably, the living room – and caught her breath.

"This is stupid. You're a grown woman creeping around looking for clues in someone's yard. Ridiculous." Beth would've laughed at her. Lacy would be horrified. And Oreo? Ah, he'd probably have come with if she'd given him a chance.

Cat leaned her back against the wall and swatted leaves from her arms. She had to get home. Kevin's rudeness at the farmer's market had planted suspicions in her mind, and they'd blossomed in the fertile soil of her paranoia.

Could he be the murderer?

Perhaps, but she wouldn't' find anything out by –

"Hello?" A woman spoke above Cat's head.

She stiffened, then relaxed a second later. The woman was in the living room adjacent.

Cat turned to face the wall, then walked her fingers up to the sill. She grabbed it and raised her head in increments. She peered through the window.

Tara Walters fidgeted with her string of pearls and pressed a cellphone to her ear. She paced to the sofa, then back to the coffee table, rinse and repeat.

Her gaze rested on the Grand Piano.

"I said, hello!" Tara snapped, then paused and inhaled. She grasped the pearls firmly and held still. "What are you doing calling me at this time of the night? I told you I'm with my family. I can't answer calls –"

"Honey?" Mr. Walters' voice traveled from further in the house.

Tara snatched the phone from her ear and pressed it to her pink blouse. "Just a minute. I'm just on the phone." She tilted her head to the side and listened, then lifted the phone, again. "I told you this isn't a good time."

Who was on the other end of the line?

"No, it's not over yet. Look, I'll get the money. I'm in talks with my associates right now. As soon as I have it, you will," Tara said and swallowed. She tightened her grip on her pearls.

Cat lowered herself a bit but kept her gaze glued to Tara.

"You don't understand. It's not that simple. I couldn't have predicted this. No one could. Look, I have to go. I hear someone coming. No, no, no. I'm not trying to avoid you just –"

"Honey?" Joseph Walters appeared in the doorway, the

chandelier in the entrance hall behind him acted as a backdrop.

Tara wrenched her hand down but ripped the string of pearls instead. The white balls dropped to the boards, and bounced, then rolled in every direction. "I'll have to call you back," Tara said. "Another time. Yes, thank you." She hung up, then turned on her husband. "What is it?"

"Honey, have you seen Rachel?" Joseph asked. "She's not in her room."

"No, I haven't seen that idiot of a girl," Tara snapped. She dropped the remains of her necklace on the coffee table.

"Are you all right?" Joseph stepped into the living room, wringing his hands. "Is this about Beth?"

"No," Tara replied. "I'm just having some trouble with a business associate."

"You seem stressed," Joseph replied. "Why don't I draw you a nice hot, bubble bath. You can soak in the tub. Get rid of your worries."

Tara clenched the cell in her fist and pressed it to her forehead. "No, that won't help. Nothing will help. Our lives are turning into a disaster, and it's all your fault."

"What are you talking about?" Joseph asked, and his shoulders stiffened beneath his designer button-down shirt. "Is this about Rachel's fees again? Is it about Kevin's? He's already working two jobs to pay for college, Tara. What more can we do?"

"Nothing. And Rachel is a low-life. She's crazy. We should never have sent her to college in the first place."

"Don't talk about her like that, and as I recall it was you who pushed the child to go pre-law." Joseph clicked his tongue and looked away from his wife. "You're just upset about Beth."

"No, I'm not. The woman was a cancer. I'm glad to be rid of her."

Cat bit her lip. Anger rushed through her again, but she had to control it this time. She couldn't afford an inquisition from the Walters family. They'd have her thrown in jail if they caught her in their bushes.

"I'm going to bed," Tara said, then pushed past her husband and disappeared.

Joseph stood under the arch and looked at the pearls on the floor. He shook his head once, then turned and walked away.

"Time to go," Cat whispered. She stumbled out of the bushes and hit a brick wall. Strange, there hadn't been a brick wall when she'd arrived.

Wait, a second, that wasn't a wall, that was –

"Miss Kelley. What a surprise." Detective Bradshaw said. He grasped her under the elbow and helped her stand straight. His tone reflected the exact opposite of surprise.

"I was just –"

"You were just coming with me, ma'am. We've got a lot to discuss," he said, and his brow puckered up. The 'you're in trouble, young lady'. Except she wasn't particularly young and she should've thought about that before she'd gallivanted in a suspect's bushes.

"I – uh, where are we going?"

Detective Bradshaw walked her to the sidewalk. "The station, of course."

Chapter 10

"Are you comfortable?" Jack asked, and placed a cup of coffee in front of her.

She lifted it and examined the contents. Insipid, low quality, just the stuff served to suspects in the interrogation room.

"I'm as comfortable as I can be, given the circumstances," Cat replied. She sipped the coffee – waste not, want not – and then swallowed.

"Good. Because we might be here a while," Jack replied. He's tone didn't change, but his posture eased a little. He cared that she was comfortable.

That didn't mean a thing, of course. Only that he was a good cop.

"I know I shouldn't have been in those bushes, but I think you'll be interested in what I overheard," Cat said. Perhaps, the information she'd gleaned could save her from charges.

She'd really gone too far this time. Typical Catherine behavior. Her mother would've scolded her for hours. At least, Beth would've laughed.

"This isn't about the trespassing," Detective Bradshaw replied. "We can discuss that a little later. Though I'll be interested to hear your excuse for creeping around the family of a murder victim."

"I was investigating," Cat said, immediately. "I ran into Kevin Walters at the farmer's market today, and he said –"

Jack Bradshaw raised his large palm and stalled her story. "Please, Miss Kelley, calm yourself."

"I'm Cat," she said. She lifted the coffee cup to her mouth and pressed the Styrofoam to her bottom lip. The white table between them shone dully beneath the fluorescent lights.

A tiny room, a camera humming in the upper right-hand corner of the white wall. Catherine put the coffee down, then stroked her forearms. "What is this about, then detective?"

"You lied to me," he said and sat back in the uncomfortable chair. "I don't appreciate being lied to, Miss Kelley."

"What are you talking about?" Cat's cheeks colored. Had he discovered the journal she'd hidden under the sofa cushion or…? No, it couldn't be that.

"I think you know what I'm talking about," he replied.

"I really don't."

Jack Bradshaw stared at her and narrowed his eyes. He opened the brown dossier in front of him and drew out a single piece of paper. He slid it across the desk. "You are the sole benefactor of Beth Walter's will."

"What?" Catherine asked. She grabbed the sheet of paper and turned it on the spot. "How is this possible?"

"It appears that Beth Walters changed her will a month before her death. She'd originally left the money to the Walters' family, but something changed her mind," the detective replied. "Would you care to explain that?"

"I can't," Cat replied. "I had no idea." She dropped the page and pressed her fingers to her forehead. A headache brewed in the center, right between her eyes. This was impossible.

She'd loved Beth, but she'd never expected this.

"You didn't know about the will? You're maintaining that you didn't know about this?" Bradshaw asked.

"Yeah. I had no idea. I never got a call. Or maybe I did and just didn't answer. I'm terrible with my phone," Cat said. "But this doesn't make any sense. Why would Beth change her will? What could have happened to make her do that?"

Jack took the paper and put it back in the file. "I was hoping you could answer that."

"Look, Detective, I'll cooperate in whatever way I can, but I swear I had no idea that she'd done this," Catherine said. She chewed the corner of her lip, then gasped. "Oh my gosh. Tara!"

"What?"

"Tara was on the phone with someone, talking about money. What if she wanted the money and murdered Beth for it?" Cat shook her head. "No, but that doesn't make sense. Why would she get her to change her will?"

Jack sat back and folded his arms again. His cup of coffee sat on the table, untouched. "You said you were friends with Beth?"

"We were more than friends," Catherine replied. She shifted the Styrofoam cup along the table. "She was family to me. When everyone else left me alone, Beth was there. Beth and Lacy."

"Lacy?" Jack asked, then leaned forward and picked up a pen from beside his clipboard. He scribbled Lacy's name on it.

"Yeah, she's my assistant," Cat said. "But she hasn't done anything wrong."

"I have to investigate every avenue, Miss Kelley. The innocent will be proven innocent and the guilty," he said, then let the end of the sentence dangle in the air between them.

Cat pressed her lips into a thin line.

"Is it true that you brought Beth bait the night before her death?" Jack asked.

"That's correct. I dropped it off at her place, and we have a cookie and a cup of coffee. Choc chip." Catherine replied.

"So, you knew she would be fishing down at the waterfront the next morning," Jack replied.

"Yeah, I knew. She went there almost every morning to fish," Cat replied.

"And where were you that morning?" The detective asked.

Catherine glared at him. "What are you trying to say, here?"

"Just answer the question, Miss Kelley." Detective Bradshaw replied, in a long-suffering tone.

Cat glared at him. "I was in bed, about to wake up and get started baking a batch of cookies for the day's sales."

"Was there anyone with you? Anyone who can verify your alibi?" The detective asked.

"No. Unless you count my cat, Oreo," Catherine replied.

Detective Bradshaw gave a small, tight smile. "I'm afraid not."

"Look, do you want to hear any of my theories? I mean, I heard Tara on the phone to some business associate, and she was worried about money. That's got to mean something," Cat said.

The detective didn't write anything on his clipboard this time. "I think we're done for today," he said. "You're free to go."

"That's it? You don't want to hear what I have to say?" Cat asked, and rose from the table. She bumped it and coffee slopped over the side of her cup. At least, he didn't want to arrest her for trespassing.

"That will be all." Jack replied, then gestured to the door. "Try to stay out of trouble, Miss Kelley."

Chapter 11

Detective Bradshaw thought she'd killed Beth. Cat didn't doubt that for a second.

She pulled up in front of her bakery, then parked across the road. She couldn't change his mind or force him to listen to what she had to say, but she could continue investigating and get to the bottom of this before it was too late.

"But where to next? Who do I speak to?" Cat whispered. She turned off the engine of her car, then got out. She bumped the car door closed, then locked it.

Tara's conversation had sparked curiosity in her mind, but she didn't have anything other than a journal which might or might not be relevant to the case.

Catherine sighed and strode across the road. She stopped beneath the wrought iron lamppost outside her store and jangled her keys around. She found the right one, then stepped up to the front door of Cat's Cookies.

"Hey," a woman said.

Catherine shrieked and threw the keys into the air. They dropped on top of her head, and she danced on the spot, then grabbed at her crown. "Ouch."

Rachel Walters moved into the circle of light beneath the lamppost. "Sorry," she said, her pink hair glinting beneath the light. "I didn't mean to scare you."

"Rachel," Cat said, then drew in a breath. She bent and grabbed her keys off the bricks lining the sidewalk, then straightened. "I'm not going to lie and say you didn't scare the choc chips out of my cookie dough, there."

Rachel giggled, then pressed her fist to her black lips. "I need to talk to you if that's okay." Her dark eye makeup transformed the young adult into a raccoon in this lighting.

Catherine bit her lip and fiddled the right key out of the bunch. Any of the Walters could've killed Beth. Or the mystery bald man on the pier could have. But, Rachel might have a lead in the case.

"Sure," she said. "Why not?"

"Great!" Rachel shuffled forward and ran her fingers through her bright pink do.

Cat unlocked the front door, then walked inside and held it open for Rachel. The young lady strode into the store and sniffed.

"Wow, it smells amazing in here. Sweet and delicious."

"Yeah, that's the cookies," Cat replied. "I'll get us a few. Then we can go upstairs and have a chat." She hurried to the counter and bagged up a few Cheeky Choc Chips, then walked to the stairs in the corner. "This way."

Rachel shut the front door and locked it, then followed Catherine to the corner.

They strode up the stairs, and Cat unlocked the gate, then the front door.

"You sure have a lot of security," Rachel said.

"Yeah, someone tried to break-in the other day. I'm planning on having a proper security system installed," she replied. "Granted, I might end up in jail if I don't figure out who murdered Beth, soon."

Rachel stared at her, eyes as wide as, well, as cookies.

Whoops, she hadn't meant to say that last part out loud.

"Come on in," Cat said, then led the way. Oreo appeared in the kitchen doorway, immediately. He meowed at her, then bustled across the hall, the bell on his collar tinkling.

"What an adorable kitty!" Rachel said. She dropped to her knees and Oreo – the same Oreo who never liked anyone but Catherine – purred and rubbed against her outstretched hand.

That could only be a good sign.

Catherine locked the gate, and the front door to her tiny apartment then walked through to the living room. "This way," she said.

Rachel rose from her spot on the floor and hurried through to the living room. She glanced around and grinned. Black lipstick smudged her two front teeth. "You've sure got a nice place."

"Thank you," Cat replied, then gestured to the sofa. "Have a seat, please. I'll get us a couple cups of coffee."

"Thanks," Rachel said, then gave another nervous grin. She

lowered herself to the sofa, then grimaced and shifted.

"What's wrong?" Cat asked.

"Nothing, I just. This couch is lumpy," Rachel replied, then wiggled around. She reached underneath the cushion and brought out the leather bound journal. "What's this −?" She trailed off.

"It's, uh, don't open that, it's just something I found," Cat said. Shoot, she'd meant to move that ages ago, but she'd been so caught up in investigating she'd forgotten.

"This is mine," Rachel said and hugged the journal to her chest.

"Did you read it?" Her gaze darkened, but not with anger. Tears swam in her bright blue eyes.

"Yeah, I did," Catherine replied. "I'm sorry, Rachel. I found it in your house, and I took it. I know that's wrong, but I thought it was a clue." She'd jumped to conclusions. Shameful.

"This is ancient," Rachel replied, and flipped it open. Her gaze traced across the word 'death' written hundreds of times over. "I know it looks bad, but it's not what you think."

Cat crossed to the armchair and sat down in it. "What do I think?"

"That I killed Beth. I didn't. I loved Beth," Rachel replied. "She was the only one in my entire family who believed in me. She told me that I didn't have to study what my mom wanted me to. And that I could be anything. Anything at all. Gosh, I sound like a kid."

Cat didn't point out that she was barely out of college. She was still a kid, technically. At least, to most of the world. "May I ask why you wrote those things?" Catherine gestured to the journal.

"Sure," Rachel said. "I did it to freak my parents out. It's the reason I wear all this makeup too. When I'm at college, I don't. I just want to show them that they can't tell me what to do anymore."

"And the pink hair too?"

"No, that's just good fashion sense," Rachel replied, and tossed her pink locks back.

"I see," Cat replied, borrowing from handsome Jack Bradshaw's repertoire. Not handsome. Just Jack. She blinked the weird train of thought away. "And how did your mother react."

"She threw the book at me," Rachel said, but she chuckled. "It's okay. I wrote this what, last year? I wanted that kind of reaction out of her."

"When last did you open that journal?" Catherine asked. "Every other book in the study was covered in dust, except for that."

Rachel jerked back in surprise. "Really? That's strange because this is the first time I've touched it since I first wrote it."

Cat raised her eyebrows. That didn't make any sense. Who would've played around with Rachel's diary?

The young girl leaned forward and balanced her elbows on the knees of her jeans. She met Cat's gaze head on. "Beth was the best friend I've ever had, including the girls at college. If there's anything I can do to help you get to the bottom of this, tell me."

Oreo hopped onto the sofa, sniffed the book in Rachel's hands, then rubbed his chin on her knuckles.

"Thank you, Rachel," Cat said. "You can keep your ears and eyes out, especially when you're at home."

"You don't think that someone in my family could have, um, done that, do you?" Rach asked.

"It's too early to say, but I don't want to disregard anything right now," Cat replied. "Now, how about that coffee?"

"Yes, please," Rachel replied, then grabbed a cookie from the paper bag on the table. Oreo meowed at her, and she fed him a tiny piece.

Catherine left the two of them in the living room, and her mood dropped through the floor. She'd officially run out of legitimate leads. This investigating thing wasn't as easy as it seemed.

Chapter 12

Catherine sat on Beth's favorite bench at the waterfront. Waves crashed against the side of the pier, and a brisk breeze rustled the leaves in the trees lining the walkway. Spray spattered against Cat's cheeks, but she didn't wipe it away. Oreo meowed at her from the end of his kitty leash.

"I'm stuck," she said, out loud.

Her cat tilted his head to one side and stared at her, but his gaze darted to the seagulls swirling overhead, right away.

The sun sparkled on the horizon, poking its orange head above the waves.   Sunday   morning.

Tomorrow, she'd be back in the bakery, making and serving delicious treats to all of Charleston.

Granted, they might not come in if they believed the Walters and thought she was the murderer.

She had to find another lead.

Cat adjusted her legs, then tugged at her jeans to straighten them. Memories of Beth on this bench flooded her mind. Her purple hair, her sweet smile, and the time she'd tried – and failed – to teach Catherine to fish.

"What do we know, Oreo? Beth was hit and pushed into the water. Rachel's journal meant nothing, and Tara's having financial troubles but it doesn't fit in with what happened to Beth because she made the will out to me." Cat hadn't called the lawyer to find out more about that.

She didn't care about the money.

"That leaves the –" Cat cut off and stared at the lone figure pacing along the pier. A man. A short, bald man. "Him."

Catherine leaped off the bench, then swept Oreo into her arms. "Hold on tight, kitty cat. We're going for a jog."

He meowed at her and peered out at the seagulls. Oreo was the adaptable kind. Running? Sure, as long as he could still see his gulls.

Cat jogged down the walkway and turned onto the pier. The man at the end brought his cellphone out of his pocket and fiddled with it.

"Hey, you!" Cat yelled.

He jumped and spun on the spot. "What?" His voice squeaked.

Oreo shifted his gaze from the gulls to the stranger, then back again.

"You there," Catherine repeated. She jogged to a halt in front of the strange, short guy, then held up a hand. She sucked in great gasps. All those cookies had deprived her of the will to exercise.

Jogging wasn't her M.O.

"What do you want?" The guy asked, his light eyebrows folding in on themselves. "I'm busy."

"Who are you and what are you doing on this pier?" Cat asked. That'd come out confrontational.

"This is a free country," he said.

"A woman was murdered on this pier a few days ago. I want to know why you're here. I'm an, an investigator," she said. A little white lie. Impulsive, crazy. This wasn't good. She couldn't run around saying and doing whatever to find the truth.

"I'm Jarred," the little guy squeaked, then stuck out a hand to shake.

Oreo hissed at him, and he snatched it back.

"Nice to meet you," she said and nodded. "Any reason you're out here on a day like this?" The ocean crashed against the pier and droplets sprayed the side of Cat's face. Oreo yowled instead of meowing. Swimming wasn't his forte.

"I'm a competitive fisherman," Jarred replied, smoothly. "I was surveying the water. You know, seeing if this is worth my time." He tucked his cell into his pocket, then shifted his gaze from side-to-side.

"Oh? I've never seen you around here before. Are you new to Charleston?" Catherine asked, and stroked Oreo to calm him down. The fur on the back of his neck stood on end.

"Yeah, I travel from town to town, looking for the best fishing locations," Jarred replied, and tucked his hands into the pockets of his faded, and dirty, jeans. "Is that all? Are we done here? Because I have places to be."

"I guess so."

Jarred strode past her and to the far end of the pier, back stiff as a fishing rod.

"Curious," Cat whispered. "Very curious. Come on, Oreo, let's get you back home to dry."

Her kitty didn't grace her with a reply. Oh boy, she'd pay for bringing him this close to the water when they got home.

Chapter 13

Pearlz Oyster Bar was stuffed with customers. Tables lined the walls and spread across the center of the large room. People laughed, joked, clinked their glasses together.

Cat pressed her lips together, then popped them free and sighed. "It doesn't feel the same without Beth," she said.

Sunday nights were restaurant night in their tiny friendship circle. They'd take turns picking the hottest restaurants around Charleston, then treat themselves to a culinary adventure.

Beth's idea, of course. And whenever it'd been her turn, the elderly woman had always chosen seafood restaurants.

"I'll get better," Lacy replied, and raised her soda. She sucked on the end of the straw, then shrugged.

"If you say so," Cat said, then drank some of her milkshake. "So, what are you getting? Oysters?"

"Yuck, no, thank you," Lacy replied. "I think I'm allergic to shellfish."

"You ate prawn nigiri the other day, Lace." Catherine chuckled at her friend. Lacy's hypochondria amused and frustrated her.

"So? I just don't like the idea of those squirmy wet, things."

"All right, all right," Cat replied. "I'll have some alone. Maybe force feed you one."

"Ewww," Lacy said and held her fingers in a cross to ward off the evil that was oysters.

"Yum, oysters, lemon juice, Tabasco."

"Stop, you're trying to make me gag," Lacy groaned, and pressed her hand to her belly.

Cat waved off her complaints, then lifted the menu and

examined the items on it. Delicious dishes, but all she could think about was Jarred Weaver. He'd definitely lied to her – those shifty eyes had said it all.

"Have a surf and turf platter, then," Catherine said, at last. "It doesn't matter. I've got something important to tell you about the case."

"The case?"

"You know, Beth's murder case," she said.

"No, I know what you mean, I just didn't realize you were that into this investigation thing," Lacy replied. "Cat, you have to be careful. This is dangerous. I mean, there's a real murderer on the loose."

"I'm aware of that, Lace. Don't worry. I'll be as careful as humanly possible," she replied.

"As Cat-possible, you mean. You've never had a real regard for your own safety," Lacy said and shook her head. She closed her menu and leaned her forearms on it. "So, what did you want to tell me?" She asked.

"I found the short, bald man those fishermen told us about."

"Oh yeah?"

"Yeah. He was at the end of the pier this morning. His name is Jarred Weaver, and he is super creepy," Cat replied. She glanced left and right, then leaned in. "He said he was a professional fisherman or whatever, but I don't buy it for a second."

"Why not?"

"Because he wasn't there to fish and he stood on the end of the pier with his phone out before I got to him. I bet he was about to phone someone or, or – shoot. I don't know," Cat said, then plumped her hair. "I just didn't get a good vibe from him."

Lacy's cheeks paled, and she shifted back in her seat. She stared past Cat's shoulder at a spot out of sight.

"What's the matter?"

"Don't look now," Lacy said, "but that Walters woman is here. You know, the wife of the guy who screamed at you at the memorial service."

Cat's insides turned to ice. She hadn't told Lacy about her late night gallivant outside the Walters' residence. "What's she doing?"

Lacy swallowed and gasped in a few breaths. "She's – with – a – man," she said.

"Oh gosh, I have to see," Cat replied, then narrowed her eyes at her best friend. "And you need to calm down."

Lacy nodded and averted her eyes. She'd been way too anxious of late.

Catherine turned her head to the side and pretended to study the specials written on the chalkboard opposite them. She watched Tara Walters out of her peripheral vision.

Pearls clung to her neck – they had to be a new string since she'd obliterated her last set – and she leaned in to whisper to her dinner mate. A man in a suit and tie, with a full head of hair.

Cat faced the front again. "I don't recognize him. Do you?"

"Nope," Lacy said, and studied her nails. She'd calmed her breathing, at least.

"I wonder what they're doing here." Cat tapped her fingernails on the plain white tablecloth.

"Maybe it's just an innocent business meeting," Lacy said, then glanced past Cat's shoulder again. She quickly averted her eyes. "Here she comes," she whispered, out of the corner of her mouth.

Tara's cloud of perfume preceded her. Cat sneezed, then blocked the next one with her index finger.

Tara Walters strode past their table – she didn't even notice them – and entered a door at the far end of the room.

"She's just going to the ladies room," Lacy said and sighed relief.

"Good." Cat rose from her seat and threw her napkin down on the table. "I'll be right back."

"Cat, no!" Lacy hissed.

Catherine rolled up her sleeves then paced across the carpeted floor and to the bathroom doors. She pressed it open with her fist, then charged inside.

Tara stood beside the sinks, clicking the screen of her

smartphone, perfectly manicured fingernails dancing in the rhythm of a text message.

"Mrs. Walters," Cat said.

The woman flinched then looked up at her. Surprise turned to disdain. Her features puckered up, and she narrowed her eyes. "Kelley," she said. "I haven't seen you since you tried to crash Beth's memorial service."

"I had every right to be there. I had every right to share in the grief," Cat said. "You didn't even care about Beth."

Tara rolled her eyes, then glanced in the mirror. She made a face and unhooked the straps of her bag from her shoulder. She plunked the designer purse on the bathroom counter, then brought out a tube of mascara.

"Who's your date?" Cat asked, and folded her arm. She tapped her heeled boot on the tiles.

"I'm a married woman, Kelley. I don't go on dates."

"Who is he?" Catherine repeated. She wouldn't let the woman shimmy out of the question that easily. "A business associate?"

Tara froze, the mascara wand hovering an inch from her right eyelid. "As a matter of fact, he is."

"I know you need money, Tara. You have the motivation, not me,"

Cat said. A wash of anger had swept her along with it. Her mouth worked before her brain could. This might end badly.

She had to control it or -

"That's right. And you've got the money, I need. Beth's money was Walters' family money. It belongs to my husband," Tara replied. She finished applying her mascara, then fastened the tube. "As a matter of fact, the man I'm with is the lawyer who's going to get that money away from you."

"What's your problem?" Cat asked. "I never wanted Beth's money. I'd give it all up just to have her back."

Tara scoffed, then took a step problem. "My problem? I'm not the one who murdered the woman for an inheritance." She strode out of the bathroom and slammed the door behind her.

Cat stared at her reflection in the mirror and shook her head. Something didn't add up about Tara Walters. She just couldn't place her finger on what that was.

"Time to find out."

Chapter 14

"We shouldn't be here," Lacy said. "This is definitely not allowed. What if we get caught?"

"Caught? Doing what?" Cat asked, then pointed at the Walters residence. "It's not like we're trespassing. We're just hanging out in my car, having an adult conversation."

"This adult conversation is giving me an anxiety attack. Do you have a brown paper bag?" Lacy asked.

"Check the glove compartment," Car replied, then drummed her fingers on the steering wheel. She stared up at the darkened residence and her heart pounded against the inside of her ribcage. It beat out a pattern. "I'll get to the bottom of this."

"Huh?" Lacy asked, then rammed the front of the bag into her face and inhaled.

"Nothing, don't worry." Catherine leaned her forehead against her window. She couldn't tear her gaze from the house. This place had become an obsession for her.

The longer she looked, the more convinced she became that this was it. That someone in there had hurt Beth. A tear slid down her cheek and dropped to her lap.

Lacy dropped her bag. "Are you okay?"

"I'm fine," Cat said. "I'm as fine as I can be. I guess I haven't taken the time to mourn yet. I just want to find the person who did this, so badly."

Lacy patted her on the shoulder. "Everything will be okay, Cat. But, I dunno, did you ever think maybe that, ah, never mind."

"Think what?" Cat asked.

Lacy took a deep breath, then pressed her lips together. "Okay, now don't take this the wrong way, but it kinda seems like you're obsessed. And that obsession isn't healthy. Maybe it's your way of dealing with what happened to Beth, or maybe the pressure of the bakery has gotten to you, but –"

"No, Lace, I'm fine. I just want to get to the bottom of this."

"I didn't expect to be sitting outside a family's house on a Sunday night, searching for a killer," Lacy said. "That's all. Call me crazy, but this has escalated pretty quickly. It's extreme."

Cat nodded. She'd give her that. "I'm extreme, Lace. You've known that since you started working with me. I think a part of you is extreme too."

"Which part? The anxiety-ridden one or the serving cookies one?"

"No, the 'bashing the coffee machine because it won't work' part. Once you get past the anxiety and stuff, you'll be just as crazy as I am. Heaven forbid," Catherine said.

But Lacy's words echoed in her mind. Was she right? She had snuck into a stranger's house, eavesdropped on conversations and been interrogated in the last week.

Beth's death had sent her into a spiral of some kind.

"Who's that?" Lacy asked, and squeaked forward in her seat.

A lone figure emerged from the massive, white front door.

Catherine leaned forward in her seat and squinted. "That's either Kevin Walters or Joseph, his father."

"What's he doing?" Lacy asked.

"Now, who's got the investigating bug?" Cat said, and grinned.

The Walters man traipsed down the front stairs, then hurried to an Audi convertible parked in the driveway. The lights flashed once, and he disappeared into the leather interior.

"Oh boy, something's happening, isn't it?" Lacy asked, and grabbed her paper bag.

The car started, and Walters reversed out of the drive. He didn't indicate, but turned sharply, then sped off down the road.

"Follow that car!" Lacy yelled.

"That's the spirit." Catherine started the engine, then roared after the Audi. Her Kia couldn't keep up, but a series of lucky turns – led by intuition – took them to the...

"Pier," Lacy gasped, into the paper bag. She lowered it and scrunched it up. "A Walters at the pier. What is going on?"

Cat turned off the lights and sank low in her seat. She couldn't call Detective Bradshaw about this –

he'd laugh in her ear. People could go where they wanted, no matter the time of night.

"Keep your eyes open," Catherine whispered, then rolled down her window.

Muffled conversations drifted toward them. The crash of waves drowned out the words, but two men stood on the end of the pier.

"It's done," a man shouted. "What do you want from me?"

Walters answered, something indistinct, then turned and strode back down the pier.

"He's coming back," Lace said.

"Duck!"

The women sank lower and ducked toward the gear stick. They knocked heads, and groaned, but didn't sit up.

The Audi started up a second later, then roared off down the road. Catherine counted to five, then sat up. "They're gone," she said. "Both of them are gone."

"Okay," Lacy said, "I believe you, now. The Walters family are definitely up to something."

"And I intend on finding out exactly what that is," Cat replied. "But first, I gotta get home and feed Oreo. He's already super irritated I didn't do my dance lesson this weekend."

"Yeah, and there's work tomorrow," Lacy said, then yawned. "I couldn't be more tired."

"I'll take you home," Cat said. "And Lace, thanks for coming with me on this one. I know it's strange for you."

Lacy's eyes glinted by the light of the gibbous moon, which hovered above the waves. "I don't know. I think it was kinda fun."

Chapter 15

Lacy stood in front of the coffee machine, her hands on her hips. "You," she said, "Are my Everest."

The line of customers in Cat's Cookies stretched to the front door, again. People filled the hardwood tables, chomping down cookies, dipping them in cups of tea or sipping store bought bottled soda.

Smiles everywhere. Except for the guy at the front of the line. His smile had vanished at the sight of Lacy's ongoing coffee war.

"I'm sorry," Cat said, "our coffee machine is currently out of order.

But how about a Cheeky Choc Chip cookie? It'll quench your thirst for sugar, if not for caffeine."

The young man in a suit and tie nodded once. "Fine," he said, then smoothed his burgundy tie. "I'll just go down to Starbucks for the coffee." He paid, then swept his brown paper bag out the door.

Catherine beckoned to Lacy. "Just put the out of order sign up, Lace. There's no point. We'll have to get it fixed, soon."

"You can say that again, murderer," a man said, from the other side of the counter.

Catherine's expression solidified. She kept that customer-friendly smile in place and turned on the spot. "Well, hello there, Kevin. How may I help you today?"

Rachel appeared beside her brother, and shot Cat a quick smile, then swapped it out for a sullen pout.

"My sister insisted we come taste your cookies. She says they're the best," Kevin replied, then eyed the array of treats beneath the glass. "I don't trust you haven't put arsenic in them."

"Has anyone ever told you," Lacy said, "that you talk like Gomez Addams from the Addams family?"

Rachel sniggered behind her hand. Kevin gave his sister a look that could've withered a full pot of flowers in bloom.

Catherine struggled to keep a grin from her lips. "What would you like?"

The line in the store had extended. People queued outside, now, and tapped away on their phones, hands up to shield their eyes from the sun's sharp, morning rays.

"May we have a box of Cheeky Choc Chips, please?" Rach asked. Black makeup smeared at the corner of her lips.

"Of course," Cat replied, then took out one of the foldable cardboard boxes. She constructed it, then took the tongs and delivered the delicious treats into their new home.

Kevin looked around the store's interior, his lips turned downward. "So, this is what a murderer does when they're not murdering."

Events triggered in Cat's mind. Chess pieces on a board moved and placed. "It was you. It wasn't your father on the pier last night," Cat said, "It was you."

"What did you say?" Kevin asked, then cleared his throat. He tried to back off, but it was too late.

He'd already gone pale as vanilla frosting on a choc nut cookie.

"You murdered Beth," Catherine said. He'd tried to accuse her to cover his tracks. He'd been absent at the memorial service. Had met with a strange person on the pier. He'd probably heard that his family had money issues, and he'd wanted to help.

It had to be him.

Catherine's stomach turned. "I'm going to call the cops."

"Cat, wait," Rachel said and darted around the counter. She clamped her hand on Cat's arm, then squeezed. "Wait a second."

"No, he did it. I'm sure." Or was she? Had the pressure to figure it out finally bubbled over, and this was the result? Catherine placed the box of cookies on top of the counter.

"It wasn't my brother," Rachel said.

"How do you know? How can you possibly be so sure?" Cat asked. He could've done it. He might've thought that Beth hadn't changed the will and that killing her would allow him to head off to college again.

"Because he was at home that morning," Rachel replied. "We all were."

Lacy stepped in front of the register and took charge. Rachel led Catherine back toward the stairs in the corner.

"What? How?" Cat asked, then blinked at the young woman. "How do you know that?"

"Mom makes us wake up at 5 AM each morning because it's good for us, or whatever. We were all eating breakfast, together at 5 AM. We have surveillance cameras in the kitchen, too. The cops know we were all home," Rachel said.

So, that was why Cat was the main suspect. Everyone else had an alibi, and she didn't. "This isn't good," she said. "I didn't do this, and it's starting to look more and more like I did."

"I believe you. I know you didn't do it," Rachel replied.

"Why?"

"Because Beth loved you. She spoke about you all the time," Rach said. "We used to watch Jeopardy on her sofa, and talk about our lives. She always brought you up. She said the best decision she ever made was –"

"Her house," Cat said. "Rachel, you're a genius."

"What? Why?" Rachel asked.

"I never thought to check out her house!" Excitement thrilled through Catherine's core. "I've got to get there. Now."

Rachel glanced at her brother, who hovered near the counter, expression torn between disgust and fear.

"I'm coming with you."

Chapter 16

Catherine unhooked the key to Beth's back door from the secret spot the elderly woman had fastened it months ago. She'd told Cat that any time she needed to get in, she could use the key.

This was the first time she'd needed it.

Cat pulled on the screen door, and Rachel held it open. She inserted the key into the lock, turned it, then let them into Beth's kitchen.

The scent of cookies and cream drifted through the house. Beth's special scent, cultivated from years of baking and creating.

She'd helped Cat learn about her craft. She'd inspired her and laughed with her. Helped her set up the business.

Catherine swallowed the lump in her throat and strode into the kitchen. She swept past the small, yellow table and into the living room.

Beth's widescreen TV put Cat's to shame. Rachel plopped down in an armchair and kicked her feet up on an Ottoman. "So," she said. "What now?"

"Now," Cat replied, then glanced around the room. "We investigate."

"Yeah, but where? I mean, what exactly do we look for?" Rach gripped a few strands of her pink hair and ran her fingers down their lengths.

"I want to say, answers? But that seems too simple." Cat walked to the curtains, then tugged one aside. Light flooded the interior, and Rach closed and eye to accommodate for the change.

Catherine turned in a circle, thoughts rushing along in a similar pattern. Too fast, too much to think about. Her gaze landed on the desk pushed against the flat side of the stairs.

"Laptop," she said.

Rachel sat up straighter, though she still didn't get out of her seat.

"Of course, the laptop," Cat whispered. "Beth kept everything on this thing."

"For an old lady, she was pretty tech savvy," Rach said, then grinned at the TV. "Do you know, she made me promise not to watch Game of Thrones? She said it was too violent for my eyes."

"Yeah, that sounds like Beth," Catherine replied. She hurried to the desk, then flipped the lid of the laptop.

It started up right away, and the CPU hummed. Cat drew the chair back, then lowered herself into it and crossed her legs. There had to be something on this thing. Anything that could give her a clue about the case.

Desperation clasped her heart, and squeezed. She breathed evenly. Shoot, she should've brought that brown paper bag from the car.

The laptop sang a tune, and the desktop appeared.

"Ew, is that windows?" Rachel asked.

"Now, is not the time for a techno war," Catherine replied. She tapped the mouse pad and scrolled over the icons on the desktop. "Come on, come one. Oh, email!"

She double tapped, and Beth's email application opened.

"Ew, is that Mozilla Thunderbird?"

"What are you, an IT specialist?" Cat asked.

"No, but I'm interested in it. Don't tell my parents though, they'll have a conniption," Rachel said, then yawned. "I wish we'd brought some cookies with for this."

"I didn't know young folk used the word 'conniption'," Cat said, and scrolled through the long list of emails. "I thought it was all about uh, I don't know. Hip lingo."

Rachel groaned. "Young folks don't say conniption," she replied, "but I do. I'm not like other people my age."

"Thank goodness for that," Cat said, then stopped scrolling. "Wait a second. What's this?"

"What?" Rachel asked.

"What college did you say your brother went to?"

"College of Charleston," Rach replied. "He did a Biochemistry major, I think. Apparently, that's the best thing to take to get into medical school."

Cat stared at the screen. Her jaw dropped open.

"What's wrong?" Rachel asked. "What did you find?"

"Beth paid for your brother tuition fees. In full."

"For the semester?" Rach shifted forward and dropped her feet off the sides of the Ottoman.

"No," Cat replied, "for every semester."

"Whoa," Rachel replied. "I told you she was a –"

Cat scrolled through the emails again, trying to pick out more information. "A what? Rachel? She was what?"

"Hello, Miss Kelley." Detective Jack Bradshaw's voice sent a spear through Cat's chest.

Uh oh. This wouldn't end well. It was the second time in as many days he'd caught her trespassing. Cat swiveled in her chair and looked at him. "Nice to see you, detective. I was just, uh, sorting out some of Beth's affairs?"

"Are you asking me? Or telling me?" Bradshaw countered.

Rachel sat as straight as a stick, hands pasted to her knees.

"I'm telling you?"

"Doesn't sound like it," he replied. Bradshaw sighed, then massaged his forehead. "You two are the last people I expected to find together. Or in this house."

"We just wanted to prove that Cat didn't do it," Rachel said.

Catherine pressed her finger to her lips to shush her.

"We thought maybe there'd be something in Beth's house that would tell us who really did kill her and —"

"For heaven's sake, Rachel," Cat hissed.

Bradshaw shook his head, and dropped his hand to his side. "All right, ladies. Let's get you out of here."

"Are we under arrest?" Rachel asked and jumped up. "Because I'm totally okay with that. Whatever gives my folks a conniption, you know?"

"A conniption?" Bradshaw asked.

"Don't ask," Cat replied, then pointed at Rachel. "You keep quiet. And you," she said, and jabbed her finger in the detective's direction.

"Yeah?" He asked, and a smile tugged his mouth upward at the corners. He straightened it again, then cleared his throat.

"Nothing. Just, give me a break?"

"You're definitely asking this time," Bradshaw replied. "But I didn't hear the magic word."

Catherine bit the inside of her cheek, then let it go. "Please."

"All right," he said. "But I'm breaking up this little party. Rachel, you go home. Your mom has called the station three times to report you missing."

"I bet she blamed me," Cat whispered.

"She's not wrong." Rachel grinned and hurried out of the room.

"And you," Detective Bradshaw said.

Cat tensed up and rose from her chair. She reached back and closed the lid of the laptop. "What?"

The detective pursed his lips. "You go home and get some rest. You need it." Then he turned and walked off.

Cat stared after him, mouth hanging open. That's been the second time he'd let her off the hook.

Chapter 17

Cat sat on her sofa, legs curled beneath her body, and Oreo on her lap. She stroked his furry head and focused on her TV screen.

So You Think You Can Dance was on again, and two of her favorite competitors were in the middles of a Venetian Waltz routine.

"The coffee machine may be Lacy's Everest," Cat said, "But you are mine."

The Venetian Waltz was the least of her worries, though. Beth's murderer hadn't been caught, and the evidence had stacked up against her. Not to mention the confusing signals the handsome Detective had given off. She couldn't focus on any of that now.

But she did.

Why had Kevin Walters met with that mystery figure on the pier? And how was it possible that the people she suspected the most had a rock solid alibi for the time of the murder?

There had to be an answer. Something obvious, right in front of her eyes that –

Cat's phone rang beside her. She snatched it up, then pressed the green button on the keypad. "Hello?"

"Cat, is that you?" A woman asked.

It wasn't Lacy. "Yeah, who is this?"

"Hi, it's Rachel. I found your number on your website. Sorry for cold calling you," the young woman said, and her voice squeaked midway through the sentence.

"It's no problem. Are you okay?" Cat asked, then grabbed the remote. She muted the volume on the TV and blocked out Paula Abdul's assessment of the Venetian Waltz. Pity, she would've like to have heard the comments.

"I'm fine, but there's something you've got to see."

"What is it?" Cat asked.

"It's huge. I, ugh, I need to think. I'm too excited right now. What's your email address?"

"Yeah, it's cat cookies at Gmail dot com," she said, slowly. "What's going on, Rach?"

"Remember how I said I wanted to help?" Rachel whispered.

"Yeah?"

"This is me, helping. Look, I've got to go my mom's going to be home any minute. The emails I'm forwarding you are from her inbox," Rachel said. "Good luck!" And then she hung up.

Catherine pulled the phone from her ear and stared at it. "That's weird."

Oreo did a mixed meow and purr at her, then blinked languidly. She grabbed him under the belly, then lifted him off her lap. She rose and strode through to her bedroom, curiosity driving each step.

She hurried to her dressing table, then sat down and dragged her laptop toward herself. She ignored her reflection in the mirror and flipped open the lid.

The computer started up. She held her breath. "Come on, come on." What on earth had gotten into Rachel? What could she have found that might be relevant to the case?

Oreo bounded into the bedroom and leaped onto her bed. He sat and stared at her, the shook his ears and proceeded to clean them with a cupped paw.

The desktop flashed up, and Cat clicked through to her email application immediately. It popped open, and the tab at the bottom lit up.

Downloading 1 new email.

"Oh gosh," Cat said and pressed a fist to her belly. She'd never been this nervous.

The computer's speaker's pinged. The email popped up on her screen. She tapped the mousepad and opened it, then leaned in and read a few lines of text.

I've waited long enough for my payoff. I killed her exactly like you wanted. Send me my money or you're next.

Jarred.

"Jarred? Jarred Weaver?" Catherine shuddered a gasp. "I knew it!" She'd thought it'd been everyone but Jarred Weaver. Or Tara for that matter.

Minus twenty points for following the false evidence and not thinking this through.

Cat read the rest of the thread.

I'm working on getting the inheritance. Please, be patient. Just two more weeks and I'll have the money to pay for your services.

T

"Tara, you horrible woman," Cat growled. "But why? Didn't she know that Beth had paid for her son's tuition? What was this all about? Did she owe money somewhere?"

Oreo meowed at her.

"Don't worry, kitty, I haven't lost my mind just yet," she said. But she had to figure out the motivation here.

It didn't make any sense.

"Think, Cat. That doesn't matter right now. Bringing Tara and Jarred to justice, matters." She darted through to the living room, then snatched her cellphone off the sofa.

She dialed the Charleston PD number. It rang twice then clicked.

"Charleston Police Department.

"Hi, this is Catherine Kelley. Please put me through to Detective Jack Bradshaw. I have important news about his case."

"Please hold," the woman said.

The screeching tones tinkled through the earpiece and Cat pulled it away from her hear again. She paced up and down in front of her TV, ignoring the performance on the screen.

This was it. With the help of her friends, she'd gotten to the bottom of this murder case. Tara had had Beth murdered.

"Bradshaw speaking."

"Detective," she said and rammed the phone into her ear.

She pressed a few buttons, and they beeped out a mini-song.

"Ouch," he said.

"I know who the murderer is," Cat said, immediately.

"Miss Kelley," he sighed. "I don't have time for another wild goose chase. I assure you, I'm following all the leads in this case, and I am aware of –"

"It was Tara. Tara Walters and Jarred Weaver. Please, you have to come to my place, right now. I have the evidence on my laptop," she said and injected as much desperation into her voice as possible. "Please?"

"Miss Kelley, if this is some kind of hoax, I will lock you up for wasting police time and obstructing justice," he said. "Is that understood?"

"Detective Bradshaw, I'm not wasting your time. I swear on every cookie I've ever baked. Please, you have to come see for yourself," she said.

"Fine. I'm on my way." And then he hung up.

Cat dropped the cell on the sofa again, then rushed through to her bedroom. She grabbed the laptop and brought it through to the living room, then settled in to wait, eyes on the clock instead of on the dancing, for a change.

Chapter 18

"Here," Cat said and jogged up the stairs to her apartment. "This way."

Detective Bradshaw followed her up at a walk, with no real sense of urgency. Perhaps he thought this was a waste of his time. She'd sure prove him wrong. "You know," he said, "for a baker, you're pretty light on your feet."

"I try to keep fit," she called back and held her front gate open. She stomped her heels on the landing. Impatience rang through her core. This was a waste of time. He needed to be out there, arresting Jarred Weaver before the man made a run for it.

Detective Bradshaw reached the top stair, then paused and met her gaze. "All right. I'm here. Now, what's this evidence you've got to show me?"

"It's on the laptop," Cat said.

She rushed ahead, then picked up Oreo off his warm spot on the sofa, and deposited him on the wooden boards. He meowed his complaint, then whipped his tail into the air and stalked off.

"Don't mind him. He's just grumpy because I haven't done any dancing," she said.

"I, uh, okay?" The Detective walked to the sofa and sat down beside her. His arm brushed hers, and she shifted away.

Goosebumps rose on her forearm, and she wiped them flat. "Here," she said, then leaned in and clicked on the email thread. "Read that."

Detective Bradshaw had come prepared this time. He brought his reading glasses out of his top pocket, unfolded them and placed them on his nose. He shifted forward on the sofa and focused on the screen.

Cat jumped up and strode to the TV. She switched it off, then paced back and forth in front of it. Her mind jumped from an answer to a question and back again.

Tara had ordered a hit – wasn't that what it was called – on Beth, and Jarred had gone through with it. Tara had clearly thought she'd be able to pay off Jarred with the money from the inheritance.

So, she hadn't realized that the will had changed, then. But, why had she needed the money in the first place?

Detective Bradshaw sat back and took his glasses off his face. "Well," he said. "Well."

"I know, right? This is huge."

"May I ask how you got these emails?" The Detective asked.

"Rachel Walters sent them to me," she replied. "She wanted to look into what happened to Beth too. She loved her. They were close. Beth even paid for her brother's tuition."

"For Kevin's fees?"

"Yeah, that's right. He was a Biochem major at the College of Charleston," Cat replied. She paused her pacing and rammed her fists on her hips. "So, Beth provided for the kids when Tara couldn't. Tara must've realized that Beth had a lot of money, and then killed her for it. Right?"

"We can't be sure of that yet," Bradshaw said, "but yeah, that's plausible."

"But that leaves the question — what did Tara need to pay off? It has to be something huge if she was willing to kill for it? And kill an amazing human being, no less," Cat said, she dropped her arms to her sides.

"I think —" Bradshaw's cell phone rang in his pocket, and he whipped it out. It was one of those fancy smartphones with the big flat screen.

The kind Lacy had nagged her to get for the last month.

"Bradshaw," he said. "Uh huh. All right. I'll be there in ten." Then he hung up and placed the phone back in his pocket.

"What's happened?" Catherine asked, and twiddled her fingers.

"There's been a report of a break-in at the Walters residence," he said, then paused and raised his hand. "Don't say a word, Miss Kelley. I'll handle this myself."

"But this could be about the murder. What if it's not safe? I don't want you to get hurt," she said, then rammed her mouth shut. What a prime time to say something that sentimental to a man she barely knew.

Detective Bradshaw cleared his throat and loosened his collar. "I'll be fine. And I'm sure everything at the residence is fine."

"All right," she said, and it came out as a squeak.

"I'll be in touch, Miss Kelley," he said, then walked to the door, back as stiff as a rock cake. He strode down the hall, and his boots clomped on the stairs.

Cat resumed her pacing. She walked to the window, ripped the curtains open, and stared down at the road, lit by the glowing orbs on top of the wrought iron streetlamps.

"The Walters residence," she whispered. "The Walters residence."

Detective Bradshaw appeared below. He crossed the street,

then got into his police cruiser, started the engine and drove off.

Cat tapped her fingers on the sides of thighs and tension unfurled in her chest. She had to know what had happened. And most of all, she had to know why Tara had killed Beth.

For closure, for Beth and the future of Walters family. Rachel was involved in this too, and first impressions aside, she'd turned out to be a sweet girl.

Catherine turned and rushed through to the kitchen. She snatched her car keys off the wooden pegs next to the fridge, then ran for the hall.

Chapter 19

The front door to the Walters' house stood open. The porch light illuminated the welcome mat and a tiny semi-circle of the wooden passage within. Jack Bradshaw's cruiser sat across the road, empty.

"Oh boy," Cat whispered. "This doesn't look good."

She had to go in and find out what'd happened, but she didn't want to get hurt.

"Smart," she said. "Come on, Catherine. You were raised to think outside the box."

Then an idea flashed in her eyes and reverberated into her brain and through to her limbs. She clunked open her car door, got out, then closed it with her hips. Catherine scooted up the path to the door, took a right, and circled to the bushes she'd hidden in, earlier that week.

"Please be in the living room, please be in the living room," she whispered and crossed her fingers.

She crouched and crept along the side of the house. Branches scraped her forearms and picked at the fabric of her jeans. She pushed past them.

Voices rang out from the living room. An argument of some kind.

Cat stopped to the left of the living room window and shut her eyes. "Please, be in the –"

"Everyone calm down," Detective Bradshaw said. She'd recognize his voice anywhere.

Catherine peered through the window. Four people stood in the room, arranged at opposite ends.

Tara Walters over by the sofa. Joseph Walters next to the piano. Jack Bradshaw in the doorway, his hand on the clip of his holster. And Jarred Weaver, closest to the window, his back to Cat. His loose shirt flapped in the breeze, which whipped past her nose and swept into the living room.

"Calm down?" Joseph Walters asked. Then grasped at his hairpiece. He ripped it off his head and waggled it. "Calm down?"

"Joseph," Tara hissed. "I told you to keep your hair on."

"This intruder has accused my wife of murdering my Great Aunt," he growled. "How am I supposed to calm down?"

"She hired me to kill her," Jarred Weaver said, calm as could be. His arms swung at his sides. He reached up and scratched the back of his greasy neck. "I did what I had to do. Now, I want my money or else –"

"Lies!" Joseph exploded, then threw the hairpiece at the trespasser.

It sailed past his shoulder and out the window. Cat ducked back, and the thing swept above her head.

"What's wrong with you?" Jarred asked.

"You killed a woman," Tara said. "You're one to talk."

"Yeah, on your orders! And now I want my pay," Weaver replied. He flexed his fingers at his sides.

Detective Bradshaw's gaze flicked from one person to the next. His body was tense, but his eyes remained calm.

Joseph glared at his wife. "Tara, will you please tell this man to leave our home? He's clearly a liar, and I won't stand –"

"He's not lying," she snapped.

The room fell silent. Bradshaw raised his eyebrows ever so slightly, then relaxed them again.

"What?" Joseph asked. "What did you just say?"

"I said, he's not lying. I ordered him to kill Beth."

Joseph stumbled back and grabbed at the piano to steady himself. He squashed a few keys flat, and a discordant tone sounded in the living room. "No."

"Yes," Tara replied. "I ordered him to kill her, and I'd do it again. She did nothing for our family. Every time we asked her for help, she rejected us."

"Why, Tara? How could you do this?"

Tara reached up and jerked on her string of pearls – pink this time. "I did what I had to do to save this family."

"What are you talking about?" Joseph asked.

"Everything was fine until you lost your job, Joseph. Fine! And then the bills came in. College fees for Kevin and Rachel. Electricity, the mortgage, the gambling debts from your little habit."

"What? I don't –"

"Don't bother lying, Joseph, I spoke to Richard at the casino. He told me they had to ban you," she replied. "So, yeah, I did what I had to do. I stepped up to the plate to support our family."

This was messy and Tara was delusional. She'd only made matters worse.

"Beth –"

"Beth was nothing," Tara replied. "She didn't care about you, or any of us."

"That's not true," Detective Bradshaw said.

Tara flinched and looked at him – perhaps she'd forgotten his presence. "What did you say?"

"Beth paid for Kevin's college tuition in full. All the years. You might have ruined one life, but your son's future is secured, thanks to the woman you murdered."

"What?" Joseph whispered. He touched his fingers to his lips. "I had no idea. I called her a few days before she died and begged for help. I didn't know she followed through."

Tara shrunk on the spot and sat down on the sofa. She placed her head in her palms.

"I don't care about any of this," Jarred Weaver said. "I was hired for a service. I performed said service, and now I want my payment, or this isn't going to end well."

"Are you crazy?" Joseph asked. "You're trying to extort money for murder in front of an officer of the law."

Crickets chirped in the ensuing silence. That was a good point. The only way Jarred would reveal himself as the murderer was if he thought he could get away with it. And that meant –

"I don't have the money," Tara said, from between her hands. "Beth's inheritance didn't pay out to the family. It paid out to some idiot who runs a bakery store."

"Watch your mouth," Detective Bradshaw snapped, through a clenched jaw.

"Are you telling me, you're not going to pay for my services? Because that would be very, very foolish," Weaver said. He ran a hand over the top of his bald head, then crossed his other arm behind his back.

"I can't pay," Tara whispered.

"Then this is over," Weaver replied. He reached into the back of his jeans. A flash of black metal appeared beneath the hem of his shirt.

"Jack," Cat yelled. "He's got a gun!"

The detective whipped his weapon out of his holster and pointed it directly at Weaver's chest. "Freeze," he said. "Put your hands above your head."

Jarred Weaver raised his arms, growling under his breath. "This isn't the end," he said.

"I'm afraid you're mistaken," Detective Bradshaw replied.

"That's exactly what this is." He strode forward, weapon aimed and cuffs at the ready.

Chapter 20

"Okay, you can come in, but keep your eyes closed," Cat said. "No peeking!"

"I'm not peeking, I swear," Lacy replied. She pressed her fingers to her eyes and walked into Cat's Cookies, guided by Catherine's hand on her back.

"I hope you love this as much as I do," she said. Nerves tumbled through her belly. This was the biggest move she'd made in the store since Beth had first given it to her.

She led Lacy to the front counter, then halted. A grin seeped onto her lips. "Are you ready?"

"I'm ready," Lacy whispered. "Show me before I hyperventilate!"

"Okay, you can look," Car replied.

Lacy dropped her palms from her eyes, then gasped. Laughter bubbled up from the pit of her stomach. The most joyous noise the woman had made in the store since she'd first started.

"Are you serious?" Lacy asked and darted to the brand, spanking new coffee machine, complete with a red bow on top to mark the occasion. "No more coffee wars and Everest?"

"I'm dead serious," Cat said. "Oh, and there's one other thing."

"What?" Lacy asked, and spun to face her, excitement radiating off her in waves.

"You can come out, now!" Catherine called.

Rachel popped out of the kitchen, grinning from ear to ear. Her bright pink hair shone under the down lights in the store, but she'd lost the grungy makeup and lipstick. "Surprise," she yelled.

Lacy shrieked, then laughed again. "What? I don't understand."

"Rachel's going to join us in the store. She's my new assistant. I figured you were already overworked, and with Beth's inheritance, I'll be able to bring her on, keep you and up the number of sales we make each day."

"I can't thank you enough for this opportunity, Cat," Rachel said. She'd had to move out of the Walters residence since the bank had foreclosed.

She'd found a tiny apartment down the street, within walking distance.

"There's no need to thank me. We need you as much as you need us, I can assure you. Poor Lacy has been running her feet raw in the bakery."

Lacy pressed her palm to the spot over her heart and closed her eyes for a second. "Oh, but that's over now. No more coffee complaints or Starbuck swap outs or mean caffeine-deprived customers. This is perfect. I'm so happy I could squirm."

"I'm glad you are. So, starting tomorrow, we're bringing out an all new cookie. It's going to be huge," she said. "And with Rach's help, we can make it a week to remember."

Lacy and Rachel grinned and walked up to Catherine. Cat grabbed the two of them in a bear hug and the trio giggled.

She'd split the rest of Beth's money down the middle. Half of it invested for the future of the store, and the other half donated to a charity in need.

"Knock, knock," a man said. "Am I interrupting something?"

The women broke out of the hug and turned to the door.

Detective Bradshaw strode into the room. He wore a smile that made the squishy, romantic bit of Cat melt. She hadn't had a boyfriend since high school. She hadn't bothered with the concept of romance at all.

"Not at all. How can I help you, Detective?" Cat asked.

Rachel and Lacy retreated to the new coffee machine and proceeded to load it up with grounds. They pressed buttons and made appreciative noises.

"You can't help me," Bradshaw replied. "Trust me. You've done more than enough."

"I'm sorry. I didn't mean to interfere in your case. I just –"

"Not what I meant," he said and chuckled. "Look, I'll level with you. I didn't think you did it from the start, but I needed to investigate every possible lead. It's what a good detective does."

"Oh," Cat said, then cleared her throat. "Thanks for the vote of confidence, I guess."

"No problem," he replied. "Honestly, I couldn't have solved this without you. Which isn't a good thing to say. I don't approve of you investigating on your own time, but I couldn't find the link between Tara and Jarred Weaver. You provided that. Thanks to you, Beth's murderers are behind bars."

Catherine blushed and fanned her face. "Stop," she said, then chuckled. "I'm not used to compliments."

"I find that hard to believe," he said. "You're beautiful. You must get them all the time."

Eggs could've fried on her cheeks. "Thank you," she coughed. "I, um, is there anything I can get you? A cookie or a cup of coffee? We've got a new machine."

Detective Bradshaw smiled at her. His green eyes lit up like the night sky on the 4th of July. "Yeah, that'd be great."

"Right this way, Detective," she said and gestured to the coffee machine.

"Please, Cat," he said, then touched her on the shoulder. "Call me Jack."

A slow smile spread across his lips, and she matched it with one of her own. No matter what the future held, no matter how much she missed Beth, she'd made two new friends. Hopefully, they'd be for life.

Catherine led the way to the machine in the corner, happiness coursing through her for the first time in a week.

THE END

A letter from the Author

To each and every one of my Amazing readers: *I hope you enjoyed this story as much as I enjoyed writing it. Let me know what you think by leaving a review!*
I'll be releasing another installment in two weeks so to stay in the loop (and to get free books and other fancy stuff) Join my Book club.

Stay Curious,
Karen Sullivan

Made in the USA
Middletown, DE
10 October 2020

21565357R00130